Life

Roberto Perez-Franco

Illustrated by Margarita Cubino

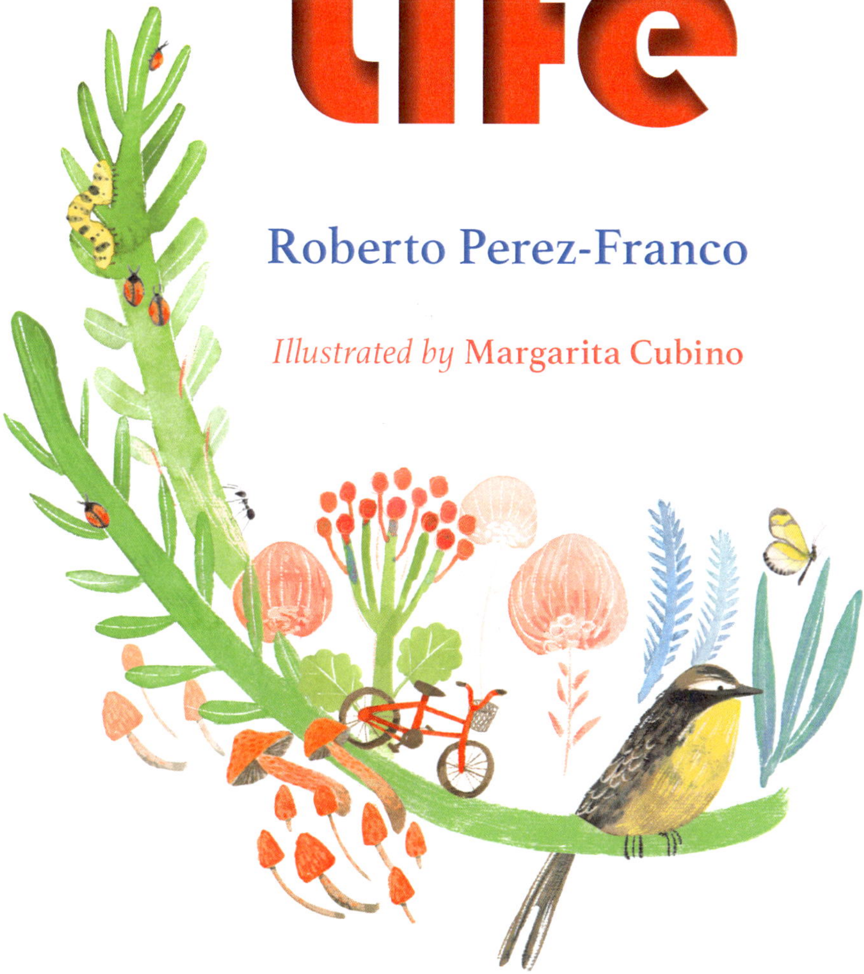

to my father

All life is an experiment.
– Ralph Waldo Emerson

The boy is silent. He peers cautiously, over the tall grasses, towards the near edge of the river. The water, clean and shallow, slides slowly over stones covered with green slime. Blending into this background, resting its corpulence, lies the enormous and majestic toad. It is invisible to the common eye, but evident to Hector, a master at spotting toads, frogs, iguanas and turtles.

He crawls forward, his knees sinking into the mud, thinking of the envy his classmates will feel if he manages to catch that beautiful specimen. "What a big and ugly toad," they will say to him. He will walk proudly, carrying in his hands the great king of the river pool. One more step and it will be within jumping reach. Veronica will look at him fascinated, with disgust for the toad and admiration for him. "What a yucky toad you brought, Hector!", she will say to him. And the sweetness of her voice will make this reproach sound like an intimate compliment.

He already feels it close,
he is almost there...
almost there...

Now!

The boy jumps like a cat, with his hands stretched out towards the toad, and falls face-first on the green stones and into the fresh water that splashes in a thousand glistening drops under the midday sun. The toad is trapped, helpless between the boy's careful little hands.

Soaked and sore, he sits up. He lifts the toad with satisfaction, and contemplates for a long time the thrashing of its legs suspended in the air. He is fascinated by its enormous size. It will definitely be the envy of the class. Even more: it will be the envy of the whole school. How lucky to have caught it! All morning —from the very moment teacher Angelica said, at the end of Science class, that they had to bring a toad the next day— the restless boy had done nothing but think about that huge and beautiful toad that he had seen so many times swimming, jumping, eating mosquitoes... what not! He knew it very well. He knew every spot on its body, every wrinkle. He knew its habits. He delighted in watching, hidden in the bush, the toad playing in the quiet river pool. It was like a companion on his lazy afternoons. And now he had the opportunity to show it off like a trophy in front of Veronica.

"You'll see how beautiful she is! She looks like a little angel," whispers little Hector next to the wet head of the toad, who responds with nothing more than a quick and frightened blink.

With great care, he puts the animal in a plastic bag, and rides his old bicycle, which squeaks over the dirt road like a wounded wild hog, until he reaches his adobe house, lost in the middle of the grazing field.

Hector arrives at school early the next day, before everyone. "Wake me up early, Mama, because I want to be the very first!", he had told her the night before, as he put the toad in an old tractor tyre cut in half and filled with water, where the chickens quench their thirst during the day. The little boy had jumped out of bed. He had showered quickly, in the rustic outdoor shower, with stars shining above his head. He ate his breakfast —a small cup of coffee, half a sweet corn pancake—, rinsed his mouth and rode off happily on his bicycle, when barely a hint of sunrise could be glimpsed over the distant hills.

Now he waits at the door of the classroom, with his toad in the plastic bag, wetting it from time to time to keep it comfortable. The toad stirs inside, restless from all the bustle. One by one his classmates arrive, and to each he shows his sturdy toad.

"Look at my tiny toad," he shouts to each one as they arrive.

The reaction is the same each time: expression of astonishment, indecorous exclamation, and the invariable, immediate request:

"Let me see it, let me carry it! Pretty please, Hector!"

And each time Hector refuses, indignant, selfish, master of the situation, rejoicing in his heart at the envy and the general uproar. A crowd of children in uniform gathers around him and his toad. When teacher Angelica arrives, she peeks curiously into the circle of children. And after the initial fright, she congratulates the smiling Hector on his great find.

"It's a little old, Hector, but it will do," she says as she pats his tousled head.

The boy, full of pride, nods his head. The teacher opens the door, the children enter, and they take their seats.

"Put your toads on the table, children."

Chuckles flutter through the classroom. The toads come out of pockets, bags, jars, and are placed on the little wooden desks. Children who don't have a toad, either because they couldn't find one or because they felt disgusted at the idea of grabbing one, move to a classmate's table. Veronica doesn't have one. Hector notices this and invites her, with a tender gesture, to come to his table. The girl gets up, smiles and sits down next to the king of the river pool, the humongous toad that looks at them frightened, inflating and deflating the dangling skin of its whitish neck. Teacher Angelica stands up, and speaks.

"Children, today we are going to learn about Bi-o-lo-gy... Biology is the study of life. Bio, life. Logy, study. Biology. The study of life. Today we are going to study life."

Hector, riveted, listens to her. And he tries to comprehend the words of the teacher, which strike him as great and wise. He is glad that the subject of the class is something he knows very well: Life. He knows a lot about Life. He has felt it very close, oh yes! He has observed it in the river, in the form of tiny silver fish. He has touched it in the green fur of the submerged stones. He has sensed it fluttering on the wings of playful dragonflies hovering over the water. He has seen it frightened in the partridges on the road, which take flight at the sound of his little steps. He has inhaled its aroma in the soft perfume of the wild flowers. He has tasted its flavour in the yellow nectar of a ripe mango. He has contemplated its colours in the wings of butterflies. And its throbbing in the neck of his toad friend, which inflates and deflates like the accordion of old Chencho during fiesta nights in the village. Life… Isn't it Life that moistens the grazing field with dew in the mornings, when he crosses it on his bicycle? Isn't it Life that burns on his skin when the sun warms his games in the river? Isn't it Life that gets stuck in his throat when Veronica looks at him? That must be it. Yes. That's what teacher Angelica will talk about. About Life…

"That's why I asked you all to bring a toad, a young toad. Did everyone bring it?"

Hector's *yes* joins in the cascade of *yeses* that falls on the teacher. But he shouts so loudly that his voice fails and turns into a long whistle, provoking a hearty laugh from Veronica. Hector turns red with embarrassment!

"So I see, so I see. Well done. That's very good. Hector, your toad is somewhat big and old. That can make the experience a little more difficult. Remember I said it should be young?"

Hector blushes again. To be reproached by the teacher in front of the class, especially in front of the girl, embarrasses him. It was not out of forgetfulness. He had compelling reasons to choose that toad instead of a young one. First, that toad is not just any toad, it is the king of the river pool, the biggest and most beautiful toad in the entire world. Second, he knows that toad very well, as well as one knows a friend, and he knows that he will not let him down: whether in racing or swimming, he will be the winner. And third, that is one hell of a toad, here and everywhere! No young toad is going to beat him at anything. It's well worth enduring the teacher's scolding. In any event, this way his toad would get to know the school where he goes every day. He had planned during the previous night, while the toad was swimming in the tractor tyre, that after the Science class, he would take him for a stroll around the whole school, with the two-fold purpose of making more people envious, and showing to his toad friend all the secret corners of the campus. For example, the storage room where the tools are kept, where the other day he found a tiny grey mouse. Or the wall where he wrote Veronica's name with a red crayon, inside a heart. Or the...

"What we are going to do today, children, is to dissect an amphibian, in this case a toad, to study its internal parts. Let's see, Hector. We'll start with your toad. Since it's old, it will be very difficult for you to decerebrate it yourself. Let me do it instead."

Hector, who was mentally wandering with his toad through the corridors of the school, reacts a little late. He hadn't listened to the teacher.

"I beg your pardon, teacher?" asks Hector, embarrassed.

"I said we are going to dissect your toad first. Let's see, bring it here…"

"To desiccate it? Teacher, if you dry it up, it will die. I've seen them over the stones of the river, dry as a piece of leather."

"Not to desiccate it, Hector. I said to dis-sect it," explained the teacher.

The boy, who had not understood the difference, obeys out of inertia. He stands up, picks up his toad —which stares at Veronica for a moment with its olive green eyes— and walks to the teacher's desk.

"Now, let's see…" muses teacher Angelica. "Stay over there, Hector, so you can learn how it's done. Pay attention, children. The first thing to do is to take this needle right here, and to penetrate with it the toad's spinal cord."

The little boy, seeing the huge needle gleaming between the woman's slender fingers, senses the danger, but holds back out of respect. Maybe it's not what he thinks. It's better to wait. Teacher Angelica is good. She won't harm his toad.

"Everyone better come here. Gather round, children. Form a circle around me. Order, order! Good. The first thing, as I was saying, is to take the needle firmly and place it here, right here, on the toad's neck, to stick it firmly. Then we'll drive it into the vertebral canal and crack!, we'll twist it one way and then the other, to break the spine and sever the spinal cord. And then we grab the toad and lay it flat belly up," says the teacher, taking the toad and turning it over, "to cut it open, with this scalpel, and to study its digestive system, its circulatory system and its respiratory system... in short, all of its systems. Ah! I brought you some plates..."

The teacher leaves the toad lying on its back, and picks up some huge rolls of paper that she had left on the floor. Hector stares at her, frightened. His huge eyes grow even larger as he examines the chart the teacher taped to the board, showing a dissected toad, crucified with pins and with its viscera exposed to the air.

"Now we are going to do it ourselves. Look here, the chart is not going anywhere. Pay attention, because later you will have to do this by yourselves, and I am not going to help you. Is that clear? Let's see... Hector's toad."

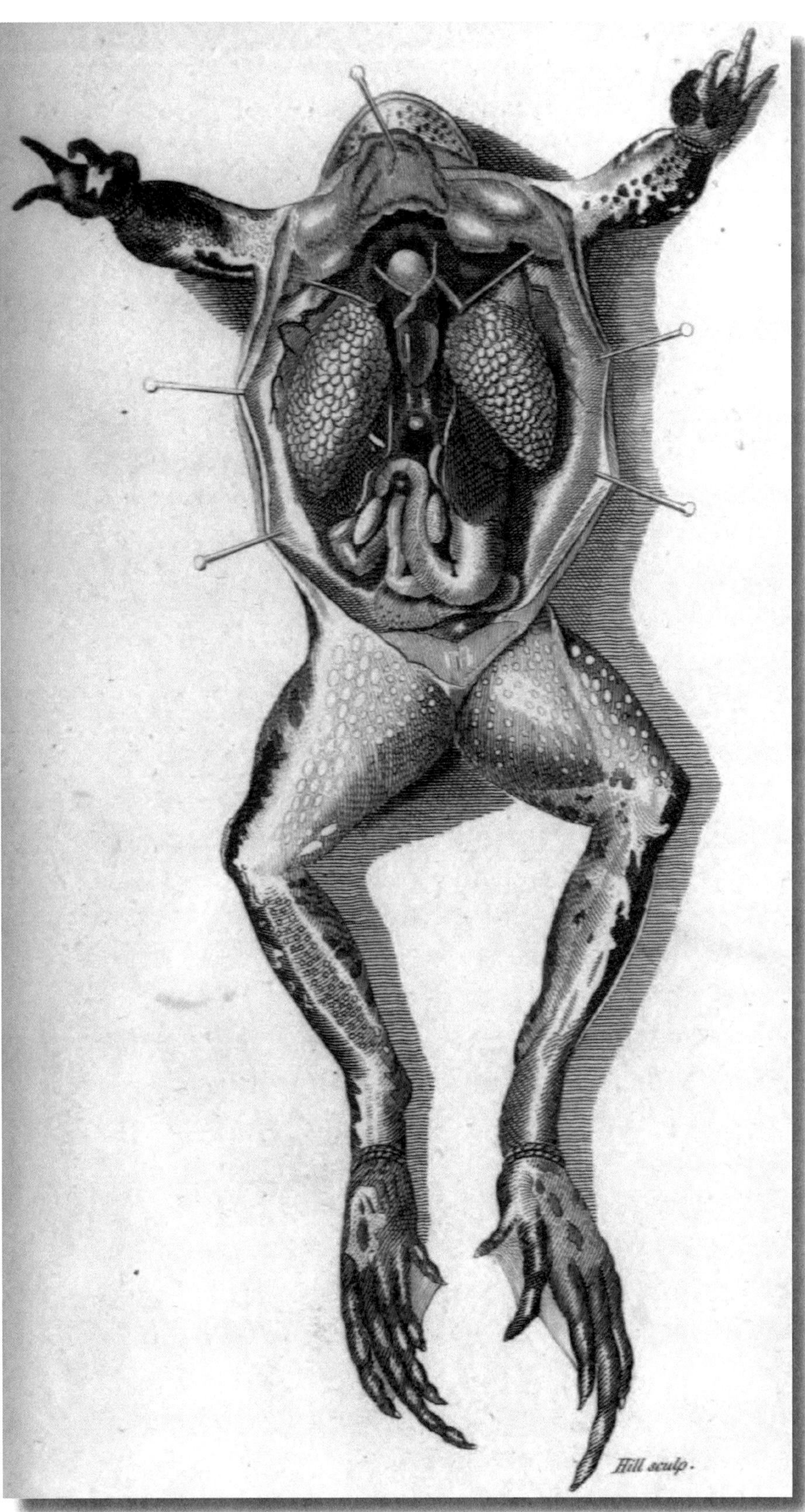
Hill sculp.

"Teacher!" cries Hector, with tears in his eyes. "What are you going to do to my toad?"

"What's the matter, boy, why are you crying?" she asks, somewhat surprised. "I told you, I'm going to dissect it to study it with you."

"But no... I... I don't want to. You said we were going to study life, not to kill my toad."

"It's the same thing. To study amphibians, we have to sacrifice some, so we can see their parts."

"No... I didn't bring him here for that... You lied to me!" reproached the boy, crying, as he snatched the huge toad from the teacher's hands. "You said it was to study life, not death..."

Hector storms out of the classroom and hurriedly flees on his bicycle. The teacher is left behind, shouting for him to come back.

N.E
Ti A.V GI.S.L
N.E.
E

The water flows placidly, without haste, in the river. The foam draws arabesques in its eddies. Dragonflies dance over the grasses. A yellow-breasted bird hops among the branches of a flowering tree. And lying at the foot of the tree, Hector admires the playfulness of the little bird. He feels a branch snap, and looks back: Veronica. She greets him and lies down next to him.

"Do you still have the toad?"

Hector shows it to her, captive in his weak hands.

"The teacher is looking for you. She wrote you down, and says she's going to call your mother."

The boy shrugs, and replies:

"I don't care." And laughing, he adds: "Tomorrow she won't even remember."

"Are you going to keep the toad?"

"No. This is his home. I'm going to release him in the river… where I caught him. Come with me."

They walk towards the river.

"They killed all the other toads," says the girl, with a gesture of revulsion: "About twenty of them. Yuck! So disgusting…"

Hector lowers his head and remains silent for a few minutes. The girl puts her index finger on his drooping chin, makes him look up, and kisses him. Then they both burst out laughing. The boy lifts the toad, and wags its foot as if saying goodbye to the girl. The girl waves

goodbye with her hand. The toad, at the first
contact with the water, begins flapping its legs
desperately, and swiftly swims away. The two
children look at it for a long time, until they lose
sight of it in the murky depths of the river pool.
They continue to stare, in silence, at the green
nothingness where it disappeared.

"Do you want me to show you life, Veronica?" asks Hector.

"Sure! Can you?" she adds, in her sweet voice.

He nodded his head. He took her by the hand and walked with her towards some wild flowers nearby, where a few yellow butterflies fluttered anxiously.

As anxious as the heart of Hector,
who carries Life stuck in his throat.

The End

The short story *Life* (in Spanish: *Vida*) was
described by the Jury of the 1999 *Jose Maria Sanchez*
National Short Story Award as "a literary jewel
worthy of the most demanding anthology, for its
human warmth, clarity, and formal excellence."
Melquiades Villarreal Castillo has said it is "one
of the best short stories ever written in Panama,"
adding that "it outlines, in a simple way, the
essence of human existence," and has called its
author "without a doubt one of the best storytellers
in Panama." Enrique Jaramillo Levi describes it as
"a kind of 'classic' of the new generations due to
its intense human experience, narrated within an
impeccable traditional structure and through the
use of simple, highly precise language… A must-
read for anyone who wants to know how to tell
a story beautifully." Editor Monica Mora —who
publishes *Vida* in 2022 as a book illustrated by
Margarita Cubino, under the Perezoso Editores
imprint— confesses that, after reading it for the
first time, she thought it was "the most beautiful
thing I had ever read in my life."

Roberto Pérez-Franco

Born in Chitre, Panama, in 1976, he is the author of five short story collections. He wrote *Vida* in 1998. In 2005, he received the *Jose Maria Sanchez* National Short Story Award for his book **Angel ashes**. He holds a bachelor's degree in Electromechanical Engineering from the Technological University of Panama, and a master's degree in Logistics and a doctorate in Engineering Systems from the Massachusetts Institute of Technology (MIT). After twelve years in Boston as a student and researcher at MIT, he emigrated in 2017 to Melbourne, Australia, where he now resides with his wife and son. His most recent work is *Essential Anthology* (2024).

roberto.perez-franco.com

Margarita Cubino

Born in the Villa Lugano neighborhood of Buenos Aires, Argentina, in 1989, she is an illustrator and designer who graduated from the University of Buenos Aires, where she also teaches Editorial Illustration and Graphic Design. She has illustrated books for publishers in Argentina, Brazil, and the United States. She began her career illustrating in animation studios for television channels such as Paka Paka, Encuentro, Nickelodeon, and Cartoon Network, and participates in collectives such as Anuario de Ilustradores, La vuelta al mes en 30 ilustradores, Arenero, and the feminist collective of designers Hay Futura.

www.margaritacubino.com

Short story by Roberto Joaquín Pérez-Franco (1998)
roberto@perez-franco.com roberto.perez-franco.com
Translated into English by the author, and revised by
Len Davidson, Erin Piateski and Erika Jonsson.

Illustrations by Margarita Cubino (2022)
hola@margaritacubino.com www.margaritacubino.com

Anatomical plate of dissected frog: Hill (1802)
Taken from General Zoology, Vol 3, Part 1, Plate 30

About the first edition
The first edition of *Vida* was prepared in 2022
by Perezoso Editores in Panama City, Panama.
- Edited by: Mónica J. Mora
- Art direction: Román Flórez M.
- Graphic design and layout: Juan A. Tarté
- Thanks to Randy Navarro B.
perezosoeditores@gmail.com

About this second edition
This second edition of *Vida* was prepared in 2024
by Roberto Pérez-Franco in Melbourne, Australia,
under his Zirie label, in alliance with Perezoso Editores,
based on the beautiful first edition of that house.
The author thanks Mónica Mora, Margarita Cubino,
Len Davidson, Erin Piateski and Erika Jonsson.
correo@zirie.art   www.zirie.art

www.ingramcontent.com/pod-product-compliance
Lightning Source LLC
Chambersburg PA
CBRC092146180726
48295CB00007B/117